AF513439

Gwen

Midnight Madness

Editorial Director: Marge Kennedy

Retold by Janice Markham

Based on Episode #27 by Marty Isenberg

© 2011 Cartoon Network.
CARTOON NETWORK, the logo, Ben 10 and all related characters and elements are trademarks of and © Cartoon Network. (s11)
A TimeWarner Company. All Rights Reserved.

little monks on the wisdom tree

Dear Diary,

In the weeks since I started this road trip with Grandpa Max and my cousin Ben, it's been a nonstop adventure.

Today we're headed for the mall. I'm really looking forward to having a "normal" day. There haven't been very many of those – especially since my cousin found the Omnitrix. Now he "goes hero" all the time, and it's often up to me and Grandpa to save him.

The truth is that I like playing the hero, too. I've discovered that I can be pretty brave – and smart – when I have to be. Here's another secret: Even though I call Ben a "dweeb" all the time, I think he's pretty cool. But I'll never let him know that!

Gwen

Table of Contents

The Many Faces of Gwen

Meet Gwen Tennyson!

Just like her cousin Ben, Gwen Tennyson sometimes uses special powers to change into other identities, including…

Lucky Girl

Charmcaster

Gwen 10

CHAPTER 1:
Welcome to the Mall!

One warm summer evening, 10-year-old cousins Ben and Gwen Tennyson walked through the parking lot of the MEGA-MALL-OPOLIS after an afternoon of shopping. Gwen read through the mall brochure as Grandpa Max carried their purchases to the Rustbucket, their trusty Recreational Vehicle (RV).

"Five hundred stores, 72 restaurants, 48 movie screens, an indoor roller coaster..." she read breathlessly. Ben clutched Gwen's arm excitedly.

"We could just spend the whole summer here. This mall has everything!" he shouted. Suddenly an alarm sounded, and three security guards ran outside with their guns raised.

"It even has its own police force," Grandpa Max observed.

"Halt! In the name of mall security!" one of the officers shouted as they ran through the lot.

"It looks like the rent-a-cops could use a little help," Ben sighed dramatically. Then, narrowing his eyes and cracking his knuckles, he added, "A hero's work is never done."

Ben then pressed the Omnitrix and turned into – WILDMUTT!

"Oh, no!" Gwen said under her breath. "I guess that's the end of our fun time at the mall!"

Wildmutt bounded across the parking area of the mega-mall. The alien mutt growled as he leaped around parked cars, searching for the criminals. In an instant, a man and a woman jumped out from behind a truck and challenged Wildmutt with a series of martial arts moves.

But before Wildmutt could respond, the pursuing guards arrived on the scene. Ignoring the thieves, they pointed their guns at Wildmutt, allowing the crooks to escape.

As he raised his firearm, one officer shouted, "They released some kind of rabid dog to cover their tracks. Get him!"

Grandpa Max and Gwen jumped into the Rustbucket and raced alongside their alien relative, motioning him to

hop in. They then sped toward an exit.

"He must be trying to escape in that RV. Cut 'em off!" one of the cops yelled to his comrades. The officers ran after the RV with their guns blazing. While zig-zagging to avoid bullets, Grandpa Max lost control of the Rustbucket and crashed into a pole. Though the passengers weren't harmed, the Rustbucket was pretty banged up.

The mall cops kicked in the door of the RV. But all they found inside was Grandpa Max at the wheel and the preteen Tennysons calmly sitting at the table.

"Are you looking for something, officers?" Gwen asked calmly. The security guards looked around in confusion and then made a hasty exit.

"Whew," Grandpa Max sighed. "That was too close for comfort!" They pushed the Rustbucket into a parking space and got ready for bed.

The next day, Ben and Gwen walked through the mall, casually sipping on soft drinks.

"Nice going last night, hero," Gwen smirked. "Not only did you let the robbers get away, but because they thought your furry butt was inside, the mall-security folks played demolition derby with the Rustbucket."

"Naa, naa, naa, naa, naa!" Ben mimicked. "Give me a break. The mall is going to pay for all the repairs, and the accident bought us a few more days here while Grandpa waits for the parts." Ben looked up from his drink and scanned the enormous shopping center. "Look at all the cool stuff in this place," he continued. "The food court and arcade, even things for you – like icky clothing stores. You should be thanking me!"

Gwen looked around at the mega-mall and smiled.

"I guess you're right, for once. Nice job, Wildmutt!" Gwen agreed.

Gwen stopped in her tracks and gasped. She pointed to the sign up ahead.

THE AMAZING SUBLIMINO
MASTER OF HYPNOSIS
LAST DAY!

"Cool! Let's check it out!" She grabbed Ben by the arm and dragged him across the mall to a large indoor theater.

CHAPTER 2:
The Power of Sublimino

Ben and Gwen stood in the crowd waiting for Sublimino to appear. Ben rolled his eyes.

"Gee…and to think we almost missed him," he said, opening his mouth wide in a mock yawn.

A loud nasal voice suddenly emanated from a set of speakers.

"Please, please, take a seat!" the voice intoned. "Ladies and gentlemen! Please welcome Sublimino, the master of hypnosis!"

"Excellent!" Gwen cheered.

"Can't we get another cheeseburger?" Ben asked.

"Are you kidding?" Gwen replied. "There's no way I'm going to miss this. But, if you want…"

"Fine," Ben conceded. "But this had better be good."

A cloud of purple smoke appeared at the center of the stage. A small man with yellow hair emerged, coughing.

He wore dark glasses and a bright red jacket that was lined with shiny gold cloth.

"Behold Sublimino!" he declared. "I am about to take you on a journey through that mysterious realm known as the mind. First, I need some volunteers."

Gwen looked at her cousin.

"Gimme a break," Ben said, shaking his head. "Only somebody with half a brain can be hypnotized."

Despite Ben's reluctance to participate, Gwen held his arm up and shouted, "Hey! Here's a volunteer for you!" When Ben tried to pull away, she asked, "What's the matter? Are you afraid you don't have half a brain?"

Ben narrowed his eyes at Gwen as he slinked up to the stage along with two other volunteers. Sublimino circled Ben and a middle-aged man and woman who stood next to him.

"Now, clear your minds," he intoned. He held a silver-colored watch from a chain in his hand. Then he swung it back and forth like a pendulum. "Focus only on this watch," Sublimino commanded. In a calming voice, he whispered, "Your eyelids are feeling heavy…you are falling into a deeeep sleeeep…"

The volunteers, however, all remained wide awake. They looked at each other in confusion. Ben shot an I-told-you-so look at Gwen. But then Sublimino removed another watch from his pocket.

He pressed a button on its side that caused powerful light rays to envelop his subjects. Within seconds, Ben and the other volunteers were fast asleep.

Gwen took a camcorder from her backpack. She was keeping a visual record of all of the places that she, Ben, and Grandpa Max were visiting on their summer adventure.

"Oh, boy! Major blackmail time," she said to herself as she recorded Ben snoring on the stage.

"Now you are in my power," Sublimino continued as he paced back and forth in front of his trio of sleepers. "When you open your eyes, you will all become newborn babies," he said while winking at the audience.

The volunteers all began to cry like infants. The man began to crawl down the aisle of the theater. The woman said, "Mama" over and over again. Ben soothed himself by sucking his thumb.

"Wow! This is too good!" Gwen thought as she kept the camcorder rolling. The audience laughed wildly. Sublimino shook his fist in the air.

"Now you are all chickens in a barnyard," he commanded. Right on cue, all of the volunteers began clucking and flapping their arms as if they had wings.

Just then, Grandpa Max approached Gwen and asked, "Uh, why is Ben acting like a chicken?"

"I don't know," Gwen replied, holding up her camcorder to let him review the action so far. "But this recording is going to be the gift that keeps on giving!"

Sublimino then pointed to one of his volunteers.

"You are a ballerina," he said to the man, who immediately spun around the stage on his toes. "You," he told the woman, "are a ferocious grizzly bear."

"GRRRR!" growled the hynotized woman.

"This is so funny!" Gwen said, laughing out loud.

"And you, my lad," said Sublimino, pointing to Ben. "You...are an alien." Still in a trance, Ben instinctively pressed his Omnitrix.

"Ben, NO!" yelled Gwen.

"Joke's over," Grandpa said to Gwen as they rushed to the stage and pulled Ben behind a curtain.

Sublimino followed them, pulled back the curtain, and grumbled, "You are ruining my performance!" He stared at Gwen and Grandpa Max, but Ben was nowhere in sight.

"Sorry! Uh, um, well..." Gwen stuttered. "My cousin had to, uh...run to the little aliens' room!" Sublimino closed the curtains in a huff.

Fortunately, Ben had transformed into the tiny alien GREYMATTER, and Gwen was able to shield him from view in her hands. Sneaking him outside, she released her little alien cousin.

"Take me to your leader," the hypnotized Greymatter said. "Your wish is my command." Gwen and Grandpa Max ran back to the Rustbucket, where Greymatter continued to obey Gwen's instructions.

When his 10 minutes as Greymatter ended, Ben transformed back into himself. While Grandpa worked on repairing the dent in the Rustbucket, Gwen showed Ben his performance under the spell of Sublimino.

"Oh, I love this," Gwen squealed. "Look at you tramping around the stage like a chicken..."

Ben covered his eyes in disgust.

"Wait, wait...here's my favorite part!" Gwen said as she showed Ben how the hypnotized Greymatter fed her grapes and then combed her hair.

Ben snatched the camcorder from Gwen and shouted, "Luckily these things have erase buttons!"

"Give that back! It's mine!" Gwen screamed.

Ben and Gwen each struggled to get hold of the camcorder just as Grandpa Max entered the RV. He took the camera and held it above his head.

"All right. That's a wrap!" he said sternly. "It's been a long day. Time for some shut-eye. Lights out."

CHAPTER 3: Sleepwalker

The next day, while still waiting for parts for the Rustbucket to be delivered, the Tennysons made the trek through the mall yet again. As Grandpa Max and Gwen walked briskly, Ben dragged behind.

"Are you okay, Ben?" Grandpa Max asked.

"I'm just a little tired," Ben replied, skipping a step to catch up. The trio approached the Sea Dragon ride, one of the mega-mall's main attractions.

"I can't wait to go on this thing! It looks awesome!" Gwen said. But Ben didn't seem to share her enthusiasm. She shook him by the elbow and said, "Ben, it's the Sea Dragon! Wake up!" Ben just leaned against a railing and gave her a blank stare.

Just then, three security officers walked around to the front of the ride and roped off the entrance.

"Whoa! What happened?" Gwen asked the cops.

"Somebody stole the motor from the Sea Dragon ride," one of the officers answered. "It probably was a prank by some punk kids," he added.

Another officer walked over and opened his hand to reveal a pale green, diamond-shaped crystal.

"What do you make of this?" he asked.

Gwen looked at the shard – and then looked accusingly at her cousin as they walked away from the roller-coaster entrance.

"What?" Ben asked Gwen. "I didn't do it."

Grandpa Max and Gwen both glared at Ben.

"I swear!" Ben insisted. "I'm not the only alien in the galaxy, you know!" he reminded them.

The family wandered over to the arcade. Gwen won a few games, but Ben wasn't having any luck.

"Can we go now?" Ben asked. But Gwen was having fun, and she continued to drag him from one part of the mall to the other. By the time they got back to the Rustbucket, Gwen had an armful of stuffed toys that she had won – and Ben had a bad attitude.

"You just got lucky," he yawned at his cousin as he plopped down on his bunk.

Ben fell sound asleep while Gwen and Grandpa Max quietly played cards. Later, Gwen was careful to climb into her bunk without making any noise that would wake up her sleeping cousin. But then, at midnight, the mall clock chimed. Gwen heard Ben leap up out of the upper bunk and head for the door.

"Ben? Where are you going at this time of night?" she demanded as she sat up in her bed.

A familiar green light emanated from the Omnitrix as Ben turned into UPGRADE.

Gwen shrieked, "Wait! You can't go out like that!" Ignoring Gwen, Upgrade slithered through the door without even opening it. "I wish I could figure out how he does that," she thought as she called to her grandfather.

She looked out nervously as Upgrade walked along the roof of the MEGA-MALL-OPOLIS.

"He must be sleepwalking!" Grandpa observed. "We've got to do something!" By the time they reached the base of the huge complex, they could see helicopters shining their white beams on Upgrade.

"Halt! In the name of mall security!" a guard shouted through a megaphone.

Upgrade climbed the giant mall clock on the roof as the helicopter circled above.

"Wake up, Ben! You're sleepwalking!" Gwen yelled. Grandpa Max put his arm around Gwen and sighed.

"It's no use, Gwen. He can't hear you. He probably has no idea what he's doing."

"So what else is new?" Gwen responded.

Three more helicopters swooped in on Upgrade as the alien clung to the clock. Then the hands broke away, sending him to the ground below.

"Time sure flies when you go alien," Gwen said to herself, pleased that she could still make a joke while worrying about her cousin.

Upgrade then swooped over the buildings and landed in the mall delivery area. CREEEAK! He heard a garage door open and footsteps coming toward him.

Sublimino walked out of the garage and stared at Upgrade.

"Who are you?" he inquired, raising a yellow eyebrow. "And what happened to the guy that looked like a walking chandelier?" He looked up at the helicopters. "Oh, well. Who cares as long as you do what I say?" he said as he waved an arm over his head, temporarily dismissing the alien.

"Now get out of here before the cops see you!"

Upgrade quickly took over a tractor, transforming it into a tank. He rode off while the cops continued to search for him in the guise of Upgrade.

The next morning, Ben woke up and found himself in the parking lot, inside the tractor's bucket, which was parked right next to the Rustbucket.

"Whoa! What a weird dream I had," Ben said to himself. He started to get up, but he lost his balance and fell down onto the roof of the RV. His relieved family rushed to help him.

Over breakfast, Ben Gwen, and Grandpa Max watched a TV newscast showing Upgrade on the mall clock, surrounded by helicopters. The news anchor reported, "Despite last night's bizarre attack and other burglaries, the mall representative had this to say..."

"This was an isolated incident. The mall is open for business. Shopper safety is our number-one priority."

"So, uh..." Ben began, "why would I go alien and then steal bizarre stuff like a roller-coaster motor and the hands of a big clock?"

"Well, sleepwalkers are in a hyper-dream state," Grandpa Max explained. "Nothing makes sense."

Gwen smirked and patted Ben on the shoulder.

"Yeah, but most sleepwalkers don't have a watch full of alien heroes at their control," she noted. Then, looking closely at her cousin, she asked, "Are you sure you're okay? You don't look quite right."

"I'm just tired," Ben said, resting his head on the table.

"No, Ben!" Grandpa shouted. "You've got to stay awake – at least until we can figure out why you're doing such strange things in your sleep."

CHAPTER 4: Wake Up!

"I can't stay awake," he groaned. Gwen ran to the sink and got a glass of cold water. WHOOSH! She poured it over Ben's head.

"Hey!" Ben yelled as Gwen kindly handed him a towel. "What'd ya do that for?"

"I'm just doing my job," Gwen explained.

But Ben was exhausted from his midnight meanderings. When he slipped into sleep again, Gwen put her face right in front of his and roared, "AHHHH!" He jumped to attention.

Just minutes later, Ben's head drooped down, and he began to snore. Gwen went to the freezer and returned with a cup of ice. She quickly dropped the frozen cubes down Ben's back. That did the trick – for a few more minutes.

But staying awake proved to be too hard for the sleep-deprived 10-year-old. Once again, he nodded off. Gwen pinched his nose, keeping him from breathing. He jumped up, screaming.

"Hey, you're enjoying this, aren't you?" he said, accusingly.

Gwen looked at Ben and said flatly, "Now what would make you say that?" She then blew an air horn right next to him. "Just be glad I didn't wake you up with THAT," she laughed as Ben pressed his hands over his ears.

In spite of the difficulty of keeping Ben awake all day, Gwen was successful. By evening, however, Gwen herself was exhausted. Grandpa Max decided that they could take turns during the night acting as human alarm clocks. Gwen went to bed, but just an hour later, she awoke to the sound of Grandpa Max's snoring.

"Grandpa," Gwen yawned, "wake up! It's still your shift."

"Okay," Grandpa replied sleepily. But in a matter of moments, all three Tennysons were fast asleep.

Meanwhile, Sublimino was plotting his next move.

"Awaken, my slaves..." he croaked, gleefully. "Awaken and serve your master, Sublimino!" He waved his arms to summon those in his power.

Ben awoke in a trance. He pressed on his Omnitrix. Grandpa Max turned over and mumbled, "Gwen...turn down the heat, will ya? I'm cookin' over here." He and Gwen then sat up in a panic. In unison, they shouted, "BEN!"

They looked across the parking lot to see that Ben had become HEATBLAST.

"Oh, no!" Gwen groaned. "Now what do we do?"

They ran outside, but it was too late. In a flash, Heatblast rocketed off. Grandpa Max and Gwen ran through the streets looking for him. They turned a corner and witnessed Heatblast melting another hole through the side of a hardware store.

"Ben!" Grandpa Max yelled. "Listen to me! You've got to snap out of this!"

Heatblast threw a fireball at him and Gwen. They dodged and ran for cover.

"Stop, Ben!" Gwen screamed. "You're under some kind of hypnotic spell or something!"

Just then, a SWAT team crashed through the roof. Heatblast threw a line of fire at them. Another officer noticed tanks of propane gas as the fire spread throughout the store.

"Everybody out!" he cried. "Move! Move! Move!"

The store blew, and debris flew. Soon TV reporters were on the scene, where a mall official was making a statement to the network news cameras.

"This was an isolated incident. Tomorrow morning, the mall will be open for business. Shopper safety is our number-one priority."

Ben's 10 minutes as Heatblast were over, and he returned with Gwen and Grandpa Max to their RV while firefighters put out the blaze. In the Rustbucket, they reviewed Sublimino's act on Gwen's camcorder.

"So, Sublimino plants posthypnotic suggestions in his volunteers, turning them into his army of thieves," Grandpa Max observed.

"Yeah," Gwen said. "But the sound of the Omnitrix timing out snaps Ben out of the trance."

Ben then yawned, glanced at Grandpa and Gwen, and asked, "But why have me steal all that weird stuff?"

"I don't know..." Grandpa Max replied. "But Sublimino sure does. We need to find him – and fast."

Grandpa Max walked over to the manager's office at the MEGA-MALL-OPOLIS to speak to an official.

"*This was an isolated incident,*" the man in the office told Grandpa. "*The mall is open for business. Shopper safety is our number-one priority.*"

"Yes, yes, I know..." Grandpa Max responded impatiently. "But I'm saying that your shoppers are in danger."

"*This was an isolated incident,*" the mall official repeated. "*The mall is open for business. Shopper safety is our number-one priority.*"

Grandpa Max left in frustration. Moments later, Sublimino walked in.

"Well done!" he croaked. "All the preparations are complete. It's show time!"

Grandpa Max had left Ben and Gwen in the mall and was soon looking for them. He found Ben slumped over a water fountain, sound asleep.

Just then, Gwen returned, holding a shopping bag.

“I’ve got the perfect solution to your sleepwalking problem,” she explained. “If you can’t touch the Omnitrix, you can’t go alien. You’ve got to trust me on this one, okay?” She dangled a pair of handcuffs in front of Ben.

“Where’d you get those?” he asked.

“Survivalists R Us. They have a very extensive selection. Now, turn around,” she instructed him as she cuffed his hands behind his back.

Suddenly, Sublimino’s voice could be heard booming through the loudspeakers. An image of the magician appeared on the multiple mega-screens throughout the mall.

“Greetings, mallrats!” Sublimino said.

CHAPTER 5:
Tick, Tock!

The mall patrons froze in their tracks as they looked up to see the hypnotist hovering above them. Even the sleepy Ben was entranced by the spectacle.

"I am Sublimino, Master of Hypnosis. You are all about to take a journey through that mysterious realm known as the mind," he announced to the throng. "There's no need to volunteer," Sublimino continued as he clung to the face of the giant mall clock. "All of you will obey me…forever!"

The clock swayed over the shoppers' heads.

"Your eyelids are getting very heavy…you are falling into a deeeep sleeeep," the hypnotist coaxed.

"No way!" Ben laughed. "A giant hypno-watch? That'll never work!" Then a bright green ray of light emanated from the giant clock.

"Or…maybe it will," Ben conceded. "Don't look at the clock! Don't look at the clock!" he called out to Grandpa and Gwen as they stood transfixed. But it was too late. Within seconds, his cousin and grandfather – just like the hundreds of others at the mall – were sound asleep on the floor.

"Gwen! Wake up! I need the key to the handcuffs!" Ben said, shaking his cousin. But Gwen could not hear him. Meanwhile, Sublimino continued with his instructions.

"All arise and obey my every command!"

Gwen, Grandpa Max, and all the mall patrons stood up, waiting for Sublimino to speak again.

"Now…bring me all the riches of this place!"

All of the patrons walked away stiffly to follow Sublimino's orders.

"Wait! Gwen! Come back!" Ben cried, to no avail.

The mall patrons took money out of the cash registers. One patron broke through a glass wall to steal a car to drive to Sublimino. Gwen broke open an ATM machine with an axe and tossed all the money into a pot.

Up in the control room, Sublimino watched through the security monitors.

"Yes! Yes!" he croaked with glee. "First the mall, then all of America! There will be no stopping me!"

Ben spotted a key shop. He used the sharpening wheel to cut his handcuffs apart.

"You may control every last person..." Ben began, "but what about a plant?" Ben pressed on the Omnitrix and transformed into WILDVINE.

Wildvine grasped the railings that surrounded each tier of the multi-storied mall and climbed up, floor by floor, looking for Sublimino. But Sublimino saw him first.

"You there! Plant guy! HEY! Stop! Obey me!" Sublimino shouted. He waved his fists in the air and commanded the shoppers to capture the fleeing greenery.

A hypnotized driver tried to run over Wildvine, but the alien managed a narrow escape. Then another car aimed at him. This one was being driven by Gwen, with Grandpa Max in the passenger seat!

"Hey, how come Gwen gets to drive?" Wildvine asked indignantly as he evaded his cousin's vehicle. Finally, Wildvine found Sublimino hiding in a small office.

"Show's over, Sublimino!" Ben announced.

"That's what you think," the hypnotist retorted. "Trim that hedge!" he shouted to his shopper-slaves.

Two of his subjects went after Wildvine with a large chain saw, but he was able to evade their sharp weapon. From the top tier of the shopping center, Wildvine released a smoke bomb, which caused all of Sublimino's minions to stop in their tracks and gasp for breath. Sublimino was furious!

Wildvine then stretched his vines around Sublimino's legs, causing him to trip and fall forward.

"You can't do this to me!" Sublimino screamed.

"I think I already did," Wildvine announced.

Wildvine then suspended the chief thief over the hanging clock.

"AAAAAH!" Sublimino shouted in fear. "Please lift me back up!" Wildvine reached out, but just at that moment, Ben's 10 minutes as an alien were up, and he tumbled, with Sublimino, onto the face of the giant mall clock.

"You!" Sublimino shouted when he realized that his attacker was the same boy he had put in a trance a few days earlier.

"I will put you in a trance from which you will never recover!" he threatened Ben. But Ben reached into Sublimino's pocket and pulled out the hypnotist's watch. He pressed the button and released a green light that glowed throughout the mall.

"Everyone! Wake up! You're free!" Ben yelled.

One by one, the shoppers came out of their trances. They looked a bit confused and couldn't recall what had occurred. But they were no longer slaves of the evil hypnotist.

"No! No, no! It isn't fair!" Sublimino sobbed.

Sublimino spotted a blue car and rushed toward it. However, just as he reached the vehicle, the door opened and knocked him down. Gwen was delighted at her own quick thinking.

"Okay, Sublimino, looks like your time is up," Grandpa Max said as he handed the crying crook over to the real mall-security team.

Back in the parking lot, Grandpa Max made the last of the repairs to the Rustbucket. Soon the Tennysons were back on the road. As their grandfather drove, Gwen and Ben sat at the table. Ben took out the pocket watch and held it in front of Gwen's face.

"Gwennnn, your eyelids are feeling heavy...you are falling into a deeeep sleeeep, you are now completely under my power!" he whispered.

"Yes, master. Your wish is my command," Gwen said in a robotic voice, trying not to laugh.

"Whoa! Cool! It worked!" Ben said gleefully. "Now, get me some ice cream."

"Yes, master," Gwen responded as she rose from her seat and removed the container of ice cream from the freezer.

"Now, give it to me," Ben commanded.

"Yes, master," Gwen replied. She then dumped the frozen dessert on Ben's head.